From his home on the other side of the moon, Father Time summoned his most trusted storytellers to bring a message of hope to all children. Their mission was to spread magical tales throughout the world: tales that remind us that we all belong to one family, one world; that our hearts speak the same language, no matter where we live or how different we look or sound; and that we each have the right to be loved, to be nurtured, and to reach for a dream.

This is one of their stories.
Listen with your heart and share the magic.

For Sylvie and
her uncle Rick,
whose capacity
to love continues
to awaken
our hearts.

Special thanks to the talented artists who contributed their time and faith to these pages;
to our Cedco Publishing champions Charles Ditlefsen, Mary Sullivan, Deborah Kamradt
and Susan Ristow; and to the team of believers at Portofino Art Management, whose
supreme dedication made this book possible, we offer our heartfelt applause.

The Elephant Prince

Inspired by an Old Nordic Tale

Flavia & Lisa Weedn

Illustrated by Flavia Weedn

Cedco Publishing Company • San Rafael, California

nce upon a time, in the middle of a beautiful kingdom, there was a castle.

Now, this castle was very different from any other castle in the world, for it stood atop a tall glass hill, and sometimes at night, when the moon shone just right, it looked almost magical.

In the castle there lived a king and his beautiful princess daughter. The king loved his daughter with all his heart, but he was greatly troubled, for day by day the princess grew more and more unhappy and no one knew why. Because the princess kept her feelings to herself, even the king himself didn't know why she was so sad. Something was missing in the princess's life, and the king vowed to find her happiness.

So one day the king announced to all the townspeople that he would grant rule of half the kingdom and the princess's hand in marriage to the young man who could bring happiness to his daughter. But first the young man must climb to the top of the glass hill, where the princess would be waiting.

PROC

Hear
hea
know
first
who
glas
bring
hap
give
half
and
hand

Everyone in town knew that the path up
the glass hill was as slick as ice and
therefore almost impossible to climb unless
one rode with the king in his royal coach.

So when, at last, the special day came,
there were only three young men who were
bold and brave enough to try.

The first was a jeweler's son who believed that more wealth would bring the princess true happiness. He cared little for the princess herself; it was only the rule of the kingdom he sought. He was certain that the mere sight of him on top of the glass hill, dressed in his long velvet coat and carrying satchels overflowing with jewels, would impress the princess, and for this he would win her hand and rule the kingdom.

The second was a farmer's son who also cared nothing for the princess, but he had dreams of becoming a brave and mighty knight. He thought that the sight of him in shining armor ridin his magnificent horse up the glass hill would surely bring the princess happiness and win him the title of prince.

The third, the son of a poor family,

had no jewels, no horse, no suit of armor.

But he was kind and gentle and cared deeply

about everything and everyone in the kingdom.

For years he had secretly loved the princess

from afar and had wanted with all his heart to

get a closer glimpse of her just to tell her how

he felt. It was this wish, and this alone,

that told him he, too, must try to

climb the glass hill.

The day arrived, and all three men journeyed through the kingdom and into the village.

As they stood among the crowd the farmer's son said, "Only I, dressed as a knight, showing such bravery and magnificence, can impress the princess. Don't you see that? Only I will bring her happiness and win the title of prince."

But the jeweler's son said, "How very wrong you are! Nothing is as important as wealth and I am the wealthiest in the kingdom. It is I who will bring the princess happiness!"

Then they both began to make fun of the poor man's son, for it was obvious to them that he had nothing of value to offer the princess. They laughed at him and said, "What have you to bring the princess?"

Hanging his head, the poor man's son told them he had only his heart and his love to offer the princess, and upon hearing this they threw back their heads and laughed even louder.

 "Love!" they said. "That is all you have? What a fool you are! What has love to do with happiness? Even if you are able to climb the hill, the princess will surely laugh at you! You are a stupid man to even try."

The poor man's son was hurt by what they had said but had little time to think about it, because just then the trumpets sounded.

It was time for the jeweler's son to begin his climb.

Confidently he began his journey,
but halfway up the glass hill some jewels
spilled from his satchel. As he reached
to pick them up, he leaned over too far,
and he and the jewels came tumbling
all the way back down the hill.

Then the farmer's son mounted his horse,
adjusted his armor, and began to climb.
He had just passed the halfway mark when he grew
impatient and decided his horse was far too slow. With a
mighty kick he commanded his horse to go faster, but in
doing so the horse lost its footing and they both slid
back down to the bottom of the glass hill.

It was time for the poor man's son to make his try.

By now the hill looked steeper than ever to him, but he gathered his courage and began to climb.

When he was halfway up the hill, the poor man's son grew very tired and stopped to rest. He thought of the princess and wondered if she really would laugh at him because all he had to give her was his heart. Maybe the others were right after all. Maybe he shouldn't even try.

But then he remembered how much he loved the princess, and suddenly a magical thing happened. Just the thought of her gave him more strength and courage than he had ever imagined he could have. He took a deep breath and continued to climb until finally he was there. He had reached the top of the hill.

The princess had been watching him all along. Now, when she saw the pure love in his eyes, she realized that she loved him, too, and at that moment she gave him her heart.

Suddenly all her sadness disappeared as if by magic. And when the king saw this, he realized it was true love that had been missing from his daughter's life.

And so it was, on that day, that the king was given a special gift from his princess daughter: the gift of knowing that only true love can bring a heart true happiness.

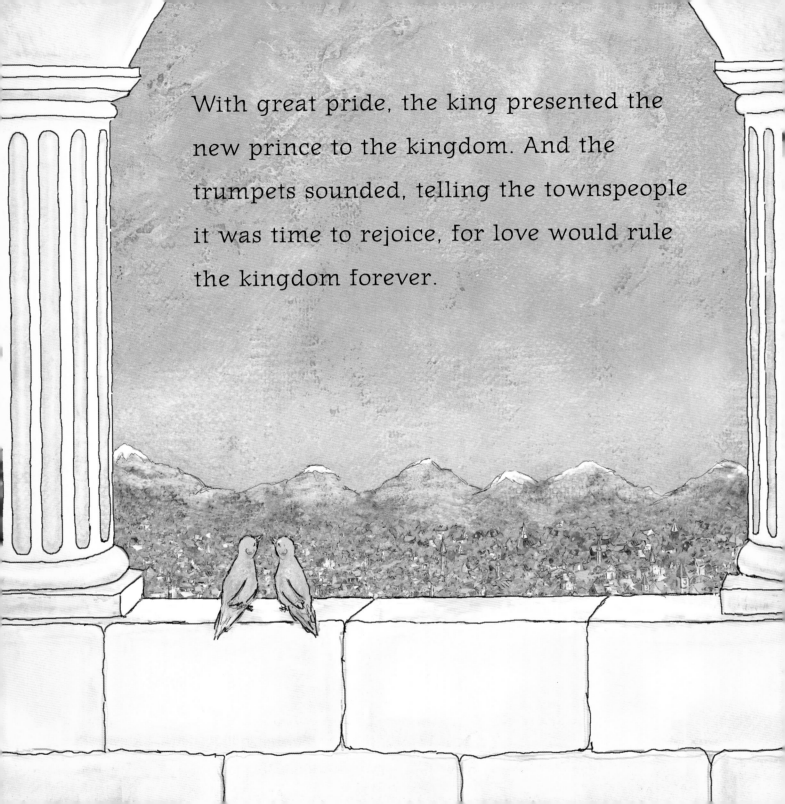

With great pride, the king presented the new prince to the kingdom. And the trumpets sounded, telling the townspeople it was time to rejoice, for love would rule the kingdom forever.

That night there was a wonderful celebration, and magic filled the air. And from that time on, the prince and the princess lived and loved happily ever after, there in the castle that stood high atop the tall glass hill.

ISBN 0-7683-2052-6

Text by Flavia and Lisa Weedn
Illustrations by Flavia Weedn
© Weedn Family Trust
www.flavia.com

Published in 1998 by Cedco Publishing Company.
100 Pelican Way, San Rafael, California 94901
For a free catalog of other Cedco® products, please write
to the address above, or visit our website: www.cedco.com

Printed in Hong Kong

The artwork for each picture is
digitally mastered using acrylic on canvas.
This book is set in Journal Text.